WATCHES AND WARNINGS

Ryan Wolf

S0-AFZ-978

An imprint of Enslow Publishing

WEST **44** BOOKS™

Please visit our website, www.west44books.com. For a free color catalog of all our high-quality books, call toll free 1-800-542-2595 or fax 1-877-542-2596.

Cataloging-in-Publication Data

Names: Wolf, Ryan.
Title: Watches and warnings / Ryan Wolf.
Description: New York : West 44, 2020. | Series: West 44 YA verse
Identifiers: ISBN 9781538382714 (pbk.) | ISBN 9781538382721
 (library bound) | ISBN 9781538383360 (ebook)
Subjects: LCSH: Children's poetry, American. | Children's poetry,
 English. | English poetry.
Classification: LCC PS586.3 W654 2020 | DDC 811'.60809282--dc23

First Edition

Published in 2020 by
Enslow Publishing LLC
101 West 23rd Street, Suite #240
New York, NY 10011

Editor: Caitie McAneney
Designer: Seth Hughes

Printed in the United States of America

CPSIA compliance information: Batch #CS18W44: For further information contact
Enslow Publishing LLC, New York, New York at 1-800-542-2595.

For my parents, with gratitude.
For Jenna, with hope.

PART I

THE

DEATH

CLOUD

THE CELLAR

"It's always wise
to worry
about the wind.
When it gets
tired of our
little farms and schools
and grocery stores,
it will kick
them down.
It'll shake us
into the
sky."

Mr. Gregor likes
to talk this way
as we replace
old soup cans
with new ones
on his steel shelves.

We sweep
the concrete floors.
Check the dates
on medicines
in his first aid kits.
Drill together
new racks.
Fill them
with supplies.

Mr. Gregor could do
this work himself.
But then no one
would hear
        his thoughts.

Speaking
makes him
less afraid.
So he tells me,
again,
how banks
and governments fail.
How they're
no match
for a good storm.

"I respect why
the wind comes,"
        he says.

"The earth can only
make new things
by brea   king the old ones,
and spinning them
                into
                    different
                        shapes."

He likes the shape
he has now.
So it's best
to keep ready.

Mr. Gregor saw
the death cloud
touch down
in 1993.
Before I was born.

"The storm
was an EF5,"
he told me once,
while picking at
his beard.
"The strongest kind."

It killed
his sister,
her husband,
        and their baby.
A sweet,
Bible-believing family
with plans
to move
to the state's panhandle.

While the cyclone
screamed for them,
they hid
in a closet.
Covered themselves
with blankets.

The evil wind
did not
pass them by
or let them be.

Mr. Gregor keeps
their pictures framed
inside the cellar.

He dug
this shelter in the ground
because of
what happened
to them.

Every Thursday night,
I help him
clean and care for
the cellar.

I wipe off
the racks of
camping lanterns.
Water jugs.
Bagged clothes.
Bedding.
Boots.
Chargers
you can crank
        by hand.

I help him
prepare for a storm
that hasn't arrived
        in 25 years.

He pays me
$40
each time.
More than
I deserve.

Mom thinks
I make only $20.

I put $20
in the bank

and bring $20
          to Victor.

My brother
could use a cellar
like Mr. Gregor
has built.

Then maybe
the wind
chasing
him around
would
stop
finding him.

He could lie here,
in this hole,
          until he was clean.

Then we could go
out East
together.
Like he promised
last August.

We could at least
get to Tulsa.
Or Oklahoma City.

We could forget Uktena
was even
on
the map.

DEAD SKIN

After I'm done
with the cellar,
I take my pay.
Nod a goodbye
to Mr. Gregor.
Sneak behind
the gas station
two blocks over.
Pass $20
       to Victor.

My brother has
hungry
hands.

They eat the bills
quickly
and return
to their pockets
    to rest.

Victor looks
like he could
crawl
into a pocket.

Like he is ready
to sleep
forever.

"Thanks, my good man,"
he says.
"Know if Gregor
might be willing
to pay more?"

"I don't think so,"
I say.

It's a summer evening.
About 85 degrees.

Victor is
wearing
his winter coat.

"Why don't you
ask him?"

I shrug.

A gray flap
of dead skin
hangs
from his
        lip.

"It never hurts,"
the lips say
as the skin flap
                sways.

"I know,"
I tell them.

The lips
don't move.

Victor's eyes
are the hungry ones now.
Sliding from
        side to side.

"The folks are still
praying for you,"
I say
to keep him here
longer.

He smiles
and the skin flap
                touches
                his teeth.
                He says,

"We all talk
to ourselves,
        don't we?"

I laugh at this,
but the laugh
feels strange
        when it sinks
        into
        my stomach.

"Finish high school,
my good man,"
Victor says.
"We'll hit up
New York.
Or Chicago.
Get an apartment."

I half-believe this.
But I was in
Victor's current apartment
        once.

It had a single bedroom
shared by
four people.

There were
footprints
on the walls
and the green carpet
looked
alive.

When I went into
the bathroom,
I dug around.

In a drawer,
under
a washcloth,
        I found
        his needles.

I wanted
to find them.

They were
holy objects.
Like the nails
that went into
the wrists
of Jesus.

They entered
his body
and changed
the course

of everything.

THE SKY

I leave Victor
with my money
in his winter coat.

I walk four blocks
in the summer darkness.
Pass Uktena Baptist,
      our family's church.

There's a verse
lit on its sign,
shouting over
the lawn:

BEHOLD,
I MAKE ALL THINGS NEW

There isn't much new
to the plains
that stretch out
beyond our town.
The native tribes
and white settlers
we learn about
in school
left their bones here.
But they hardly changed
the land.

Maybe Mr. Gregor
is wrong
about the earth
making new things
after the storms.

Our wooden houses
keep cozy and quiet.
But they don't
belong here.
The cyclones only
bring the land
back
to what it was
before.

The sky wants
the land
to stay flat.
That way
its beauty
doesn't compete
with our little buildings.
The sky can stay pure
on a clear day
or a cloudless night.

Tonight
the sky
is black.

BLESSING

I enter
my home
through the back door.

I give my mom
$20
to put into
the bank.
Place the bill
in her palm
without looking up
at her face.

I begin
setting
the table.

      Fork, knife, spoon.
            Fork, knife, spoon.
                  Fork, knife, spoon.

And a tiny pink spoon
      for Angeline.

Mom
gets Angeline
snug
into her high chair.

Dad pours
grape juice
into our glasses.

Chicken sizzles.
Broccoli steams.

We pray
for my sister
and
for my brother.

We take turns.

If it's
Dad's turn,
he always
clears
his throat.

He speaks
the same way he does
when leading prayer
          during Sunday School
          and on
          Warrior Wednesdays.

He has a firm voice
that lands
like a gavel,
insisting God has
                    no choice
                    but to listen.

When it's
Mom's turn,
she sounds
like she's put makeup
on her voice.

It's the voice
she wears
when leading prayer
        during Sunday School
        and on
        Warrior Wednesdays.

My parents
are youth pastors.
A husband
and wife
team.

Their voices
must stay
bright enough
to keep teenagers
        awake.

Last year,
they chose
to show our church
how large
their hearts were.

They adopted
a child
with Down syndrome
from South Korea.
Named her Angeline
after my grandmother
who died
of lung cancer.

We pray
for Angeline's
upcoming doctor's visits.
For her health
and happiness.
That she grows up
      strong,
knowing she is
      loved.
For not only
is she their child,
      she is God's child.

Angeline likes
      to wave
      her arms
during the prayer.

Later,
I'll wipe
   drool
off
her high chair tray.

We pray
for Victor.
For his safety
and return.
That he is healed
of the sickness
in his body
        and soul.
Released from
the hold
Satan has
on his life.
Receives the help
he needs
to be made
        whole.

His chair
sits empty
across from me.

He is alive,
for now.
Still, I imagine
his ghost is seated
with us.

During the middle
of the prayer,
Mom checks
to see if my eyes are
shut.

Sometimes
if it's her turn to pray,
she says,
"Lord, I hope Philip
will show respect by
keeping
his
lids
closed
and his heart on
                    You."

It's funny.
She has to open
her own eyes
to know mine
                aren't shut.

When I pray,
I tend to mumble.
But I'm sure to cover
the important bits.

And no matter
who is speaking,
we always end with:

Bless this food to our bodies.
Keep Your angels
around us.

In Your precious name,

                    Amen.

20

THE AX

I go to bed early
on a summer night
while others
my age
are elsewhere.
Some must be
drinking in secret
at friends' houses.
Or kissing their dates
with open mouths.

They must be
forgetting
about death.

Victor liked to smile
at death.

He used to show me
horror movies
          on his laptop
while my parents
slept.

Our beds were both
          in this room.

I sat on
his mattress.

He picked out
a video,
illegally downloaded.

We watched
teenage actors
who could barely say
their lines
get their
eyes poked out.
Necks stabbed.
Throats slit.

We laughed.

Once,
when an ax
went into the head
of some drunk kid,
I asked,
"Do you think he went
        to heaven
        or hell?"

I was 12 years old.
The question
seemed fair.

"He didn't go
anywhere,"
Victor said,
smiling.

"The ax comes
toward your face,
     then Nothing.
You don't remember
it hitting you.
     It's like it
     never came
     and you
     never were."

This confused me.

What my parents said
about heaven
was "gospel truth."
But Victor was smart.
He knew things
Mom and Dad didn't.

The thought
of that kind
     of death
made me feel
cold and small.
I tried to imagine
everything I was
coming to a
          stop.

I couldn't
do it.
Still don't
     know
     how to.

Since that night,
I always think about
death
before I fall
asleep.

I used to try
to picture
        Nothingness.

I only saw
the color black.
Which is not
the same
as Nothingness.

Now sometimes,
when I think of death,
I picture Victor
at 16
with the wrist he
        broke
while playing football.

He is lying on the couch,
with his working hand
        at rest
        in a potato chip bag
        for an entire hour,
        staring
        at a
        blank
        television
        screen.

He doesn't seem
happy
    or hurt.

He doesn't seem
like
anything.

Later,
I find out
he's taken
    five Percocet pills
    for his pain.

He only needed
one.

This could be
        how death is.

You just stay
like Victor was.

Frozen
    forever.

For now,
I am here.
In this bed.
My thoughts
slow,
but do not
    stop.

I hear
the rain on the rooftop.
Feel the sheets
around me.
Taste the mint
from my toothpaste.
Smell the damp dust
in the air.
Some of it made
of my own
dead
skin.

I forget
where I am
and
that I am,
in the end.

I dream
about
Mr. Gregor's
storm cellar.

I am packing
cans of soup
onto the shelves,
but every time
I look back,

the shelves are empty.

WATCH

I come out
of the fog
at 1 a.m.
to thunder
slapping the sky.
Rain on the rooftop
landing louder.

My phone
buzzing.

A text alert.

Tornado watch
for the county.

This is the fourth
tornado watch
this year.
Two tornadoes
touched ground
last month.
But they were
weak
and neither
reached
Uktena.

The wind
rushes
in wild bursts.
Pressing itself
against the house.
Breathing hard
onto the walls.

I wonder
about the thunder.
The wind
and the rain.
Try to remember
the steps to the science
behind
the sounds.

I am not afraid,
only curious
and
a bit
tired.

My thoughts
        sink.

I float back
into
    sleep.

WARNING

A hand is shaking
            my shoulder.
The fingers
dig me up
from a dream
I am forgetting.

"Tornado warning,"
Dad says,
his voice pulling
at my ears.
"It's plenty bad
out there."

My bare feet
trade damp sheets
for carpet.

The wind
is beating at
the side of the house
even harder now.
Each gust
comes in waves
along the floor.

The storm siren
lives near
my high school.

I can make out
its whine along
with the wind.
It moves with
the gusts.

"Your mom
and Angeline
are in the basement,"
Dad says.

We are lucky.
Most homes in Uktena
        don't have basements
because of the soil here.

Lightning flashes
through my blinds.
It washes over the bed,
        where I am
            no longer lying.

The room returns
to darkness.

Dad tosses me
a hooded sweatshirt
that belonged
to my brother.

I wonder if Victor
is shooting up
in his bathroom
right now.

As a storm rages outside,
he will push
a stronger storm
                    into
                    his
                    blood.

I look back
at my bedroom
as we leave it.

On my dresser,
I see the shadow-shapes
of model helicopters.

Victor and I
built them together,
        years ago.

I remember how
tough it was
to wash
the model cement
from my fingers.

Another
flash.

A sudden anger
jumps
into my throat.

I want the bed that
keeps me warm
to burn.

    I want the walls
    to be taken
    by the wind.

        I want to be
        shaken
        into the sky.

The feeling
leaves me,
quick as it came.
Shivers
replace it.

The thunder
rumbles
along the hairs
on my arms.

I follow
my father
    downstairs.

Fear crackles
under my tongue
as we cross the kitchen.

We enter
the open
basement door.

THE BASEMENT

We are on the stairs
when the lights go
out.

Angeline's
scream
scrapes
the total black.

I feel around for
the rail.
Still trip
on the last step.

I move toward
the sound of
the NOAA Weather Radio,
running on battery.
Toward Mom singing to Angeline:
> *"He's got the whole world*
> *in His hands..."*

Dad swears
as his foot
strikes something
in the dark.

I've never heard
him curse before.

The radio is repeating
the same warning
on a loop.

Take
immediate
cover.

Angeline and Mom
are huddled
under the table
with the radio on it.
When I reach them,
I grab Angeline's shoulder
by accident.

She screams again.

"*Sssshhhh,*"
Mom says.
"*Sssshhhh.*
It's okay, baby.
It's okay."

She sings,
more slowly than
in church.

She prays.

The prayer is not
forced
like a church prayer
        or a dinner prayer.

It's a prayer that
shivers in the dark.
Like the feeling
I had in my bedroom.

My mother
seems more sad
and real to me
than I can remember.

I would answer
her prayer
            if I had the power.

I think of
Mr. Gregor's sister
and her baby
in 1993.

Did they sing
            into the storm?

Did they pray?

I try to.
But only in my head
with its broken
            thoughts.
And not for
very long.

My eyes
fill with
white.

Dad's pointing
a flashlight
he found in a drawer.

I see the
wet cheeks
of my mom
and Angeline.

> *Take*
> > *immediate*
> > > *cover.*

The flashlight
lowers.

There's a buzz
and a rattle.
The careless footsteps
of a greedy giant
in a fairy tale.

My ears
begin to
pop
and I know
what this
means.

The
death
cloud.

The ax.

PRESSURE

The flashlight
streaks
    and scratches
        along the darkness.

A roar
covers
everything.

In bursts,
I see the basement's
beams and boxes,
the washer, the dryer,
tables,
    chairs,
                all jumping
    old toy sets,   like popcorn.

    Like the ground
        is covered in hot coals.

The radio voice whirrs
    as it bounces from the table
and   breaks
    onto the concrete.
Angeline's child-screams
combine with
        Mom's prayers
        inside
        the roar.

Dad   trips
        as he dives
under the table
with us.
His shoulder
         pushes
against mine.

The hiss and the crash,
above   and   around,
       drown
             my ears.

The pressure
   pulls
    me
   down
  into a pit
inside myself.

My mind is a room
inside a room and
the room is full.
So full that there
is no empty space
at all.

I cannot move.

Everything
around me
is slow
and heavy.

Time
      is twisted up
in the death cloud.
      It stretches with
                the roar.

Then the cloud

lets

it

go.

Time drops
onto the floor.

Returns to
its usual flow.

Angeline's little voice
is full
of baby tears
      and we are not dead.

We are
not dead.

Nothing has stopped.

Dad's flashlight
shows us
the basement now.

White dust
has fallen
from the ceiling.
But the ceiling is still there.

The washer and dryer
moved
a few inches,
but aren't dented.

Cardboard boxes
slipped
from their shelves.
But the shelves stand firm.

Mom is kissing Angeline
over
and over.

Dad just keeps
moving his flashlight,
back–forth,
        forth–back,
across the room.

"Thought there
would be
more damage,"
he says.
"It sounded
so close."

I want to check
my phone
to see if
the twister is gone.

I feel for it.
In the hoodie.
In my sweatpants.
Must have left it
on my bed.

"You got
your phone, Dad?"
I ask.

"Yes,"
he says.
"Should've just
used its light
before.
Wasn't
thinking."

"Check the
alerts,"
I say.

He turns
off the flashlight.
The basement
goes dark again.

I can feel
the heat of our life,
      hanging in the black.

Dad's phone screen
brightens
the room.

"I think
we're fine,"
he says
after a long minute.

Angeline
is quiet now.

"I think
we're fine."

THE BALCONY

There's more
white dust
upstairs.

Shards
from a glass
left on the counter
dot the kitchen floor.

The window is
cracked
over our sink.
Through it,
I see the night sky
tinted green.

The lime glow
spreads across
a dim collage
of metal and wood.

Streetlights
and power lines
        are snapped.
Wooden poles
        crisscrossed.

Branches
from trees in separate yards
make bony
      handshakes.

Houses are tilted,
      poked by the finger
of the fairy-tale giant.

The homes of
the Fischers,
      a young couple,
and the Wagners,
      a family of four,
aren't there
      at all.

There is
a view to the plains
where their houses
stood.
Crooked posts
      stick out from
uneven ground.

I tremble.
Feel a gust
come from the staircase
going up to
the bedrooms.

When I turn,
the wind reaches
under my hood.
Glides along the sides
of my neck.

I hear Dad
curse again
as he walks past me.

I follow him
        upstairs.

In my parents' bedroom,
a table lamp
        is broken.
A jewelry box
        has spit out its rings
        and necklaces.
Angeline's pink crib
is closer
to the television
than before.

But the walls
are unmoved.
The rosy wallpaper
unpeeled.

Across the hall,
my door is
thrown open.
Barely on
      its hinges.

Wind cuts
through the gap.
A light spray
of rain
travels with it.

Faint green from
the after-storm
shines sickly
on the doorframe.

Two of my
bedroom walls
      are pushed away.
So is a chunk
of the ceiling.
Gone into
the green night.

I have
a new balcony.

It holds
a perfect view
of Uktena.

The wicked wind
granted the wish
    I never
    should
    have had.

The death cloud
shook
my room
into sky.

    Tossed
    my bed
    to the trees.

It's brought
a new guest
to take my place.

The guest
    is lodged
into the side
of a wall
that still exists.

Where
model helicopters
once perched
is the sign
from our church.

Its message
looks like a
Wheel of Fortune puzzle.

Letters
are missing.
But I can fill in
the blanks:

BEH_LD,
I MAK_   A_L TH_NGS N_W

PART II

THE

TAR

PIT

THE DOOR'S EDGE

The death cloud
took Mr. Gregor.
Slammed him
into the doors
of his cellar
as he tried
to get underground.

When he was found
the next day,
his head
was nearly pulled
from his neck.
The corner of a door
had jammed
into his throat.
Turned his tongue
        to red mush.

No one knew why
Mr. Gregor
was not already
inside his cellar
after the first storm watch
was issued.

He always listened
to the radio.
Played it at
his bedside
through the night.

He should've
heard the warning.

His house
fell directly within
the tornado's
warpath.
It was beaten
into a pile
of planks.

I never saw
the result.
Dad wouldn't let me
come along
when he surveyed
the neighborhood
to see how bad
        the damage was.

He went with
a police officer
who visited
my school once
to talk about the dangers
of drugs.

When they found
Mr. Gregor's body,
they carried it
for half a mile.
Ambulances
couldn't get
any closer.

Our streets
are twisted forests
bunched with wire.

Uktena is near
the plains.
Yet there are woods
along the border.
Most who built
their homes here
grew even more trees
in their yards.

Some that fell
during the storm
were over
100 years old.

Their long trunks
lie through
the middle
of every road
into town.

The National Guard
was called in
to help with
the recovery.
Only a few trucks
have arrived.
They park
outside
our forest streets.

Other towns
have worse damage.
If that is even
possible.

All day,
I hear neighbors
with chainsaws
        cutting apart branches
        and tree trunks.

They wade through
the wires
and metal scraps.
Clear away brush.

When I hear the saws,
I think of
the door's edge,
        cutting into
        Mr. Gregor.

I wonder
how he felt
in that instant.
A horror film
come to life.

It wasn't
a masked killer
or hateful ghost
        snatching his soul.

It was the earth itself,
as Mr. Gregor
expected.

It took him to join
        his sister,
        her husband,
        his baby nephew.

Sometimes
I almost believe
if I think
about death
for long enough,
I will never
die.

But that
doesn't work.

Thinking about death
didn't save
Mr. Gregor.

It's silly,
but I wish
I'd tugged on
his beard.
Just to know
     how real
     he was.

I've clawed at the skin
on my arm
to feel
my own realness.

The feeling
doesn't stick.

The death cloud's
shadow
makes everything
     unreal.

It pushes life
to become
stranger
and stranger.

Last night,
Victor came
home.

RETURN

Two nights
after the storm,
the doorbell rang.
We are still
without power,
but the bell
doesn't seem to
need it.

Dad greeted Victor
like the prodigal son
in the Book of Luke.
Unlike the Bible story,
we couldn't throw
        a feast.
We'd already cooked
our meat
on a gas grill.
Otherwise,
it would've spoiled.

Victor is unable
to hold down food
anyhow.

He wouldn't enjoy
our dry cereal.
The few apples
that stayed fresh.

Victor is
the opposite of fresh.
The dead skin
on his lips
blends
into the rest
of his bloodless face.

When he stepped into
our hallway
for the first time
in over a year,
Mom kissed
his clammy cheek.
Dad rubbed
his shoulders.
They said
a prayer of thanks.

Angeline was
sitting nearby
in a playpen.
She stared
with her curious child-eyes
at the stranger
who had entered.
Put a plush cube
in her mouth
        and drooled.

Victor looked
back at her.
Tried to make a face
he must have thought
        was cute.

It was painful.
As if the
muscles in his face
        were rusted
        and worn.

Mom and Dad
spilled smiles
everywhere.

Acted like
their house
wasn't missing a room.

Like their oldest son
wasn't actually
a junkie
they'd kicked out
themselves.

Like Victor
was coming home
from college
in another state.
Instead of from a dump
        a mile across town.

I should share
this happiness.

But I feel my face
turning into Victor's
just
by
looking at him.

I've wanted to cross
the country
with him.
Live out
the adventures
he promised
in a brighter world
that isn't here.

But we are here.
In this home.
Where we were children.

And Victor
can never
be a child
again.

VICTOR SAYS

Victor is drained,
all weak and wispy.
Hard to imagine
he ever played football
in high school.

He still likes to
talk though,
pacing as he speaks.
Sometimes
he sits down,
gagging and gasping,
then stands back up.
Paces again.

He chews on his lips.
Scratches
the back
of his neck.
Tells us
"the whole awful
everything."

It's like he wants
his secrets
to be spun
into gold
that might buy
his family's favor.

Victor says
he heated,
        then shot up,
the last
of his supply
during the tornado.

His roommates
joined in.

They sat in the dark.
Heard the storm
flow
around
their walls.

Victor thought
it was
a good moment
        to dissolve.

He wanted
        to drift off
                into the wind.

But within hours,
he was sober.

The storm
had turned to
a cloudless dawn.

He felt a ticking
in his muscles.
Tasted
the sharp bite
of acid
coming up
from his stomach.

His friends
were ready
to score
their next hit.
After looking out
at the parking lot,
they realized
what the storm
thought of their plans.

They'd been driving
to Tulsa.
Picking up
quarter-sized balloons
of black paste
called "Tar."

Only Big Gabe,
the tallest
of Victor's roommates,
had a vehicle.
It was an old
Dodge Tradesman van
his father gave him.

The Tradesman was
        upside-
                down.
Engine plucked
from the vehicle.
Sprinkled in pieces
        around
            the property.

Seeing this,
the entire apartment
        erupted.

Closets were
        searched.
Drawers thrown
        into walls.
No traces
of leftover Tar
were found.

After almost 24 hours
without a hit,
Victor was turning
        to
        sweat.

The sweat was
                hot-cold
            cold-hot.
Left him seasick
from the
        shifting.

Soon
he was vomiting
all over
the bedroom.

    Throwing up
    before
    he could reach
    the toilet.

He puked
until there was
no acid
    left
in his stomach.

His friends
were similar messes
of sweat and vomit.

They called for
a pill patrol.

Everyone went
outside,
into dizzy air
that smelled of
sawdust
and gasoline.
There were people
in the streets.
Moving debris.
Looking for things
    they had lost.

It was hard to find
a house
to break into
without being seen.
Even if the homes
were already
        half-broken
by the storm.

When they did
crawl through
a few
smashed windows,
there was
nothing stronger
than Tylenol
in the medicine cabinets.

They took
extra doses of it.
Didn't fix
        the ache.

In one home,
they were nearly caught.
A little girl
in blue pajamas
walked into the bathroom,
rubbing
        her eyes.

Tiny cuts
from what looked
like glass
surrounded
her eyebrows.

She started screaming
just as Victor
        jumped
out of the window
and onto
        an uprooted shrub.

Between break-ins,
he and his friends
called everyone
they knew.

Perhaps there was
a connection
willing to drive
out from Tulsa.
Meet them at
the edge of town.

Their phones died
before they even
landed
        a *maybe*.

Victor sat down
at a bench
in what was once
a mobile home's backyard.

The home itself
was on its side
        across the street.

While his friends swore
and smoked cigarettes,
he shut
his eyes.

When he awoke
from a sleep
he wasn't sure
was sleep at all,
they were gone.

A dark-haired, mud-spotted dog
was licking
        his chin.

The mutt was chubby
and well-fed,
but limped from
a gash
in his leg.

There was no sign
of an owner.

Victor didn't care
to read
the collar.

He wanted
to kick
the creature away.
Didn't
let himself
fall
that far.

He felt a drive
to move forward.
An odd energy
        turning within
his hollow
gut.

He'd go
home now.
Beg forgiveness.
Kiss the carpet
of the house
he grew up in.

If he was going to
detox,
if he was going
        to get clean,
he wanted to do it
this way.

At home,
with the people
who gave him
life.

Who probably
loved him.

In some sense,
at least.

Tonight,
I share the living room
with my brother.

Dad considered
walking him to the
border of Uktena
and calling an ambulance.

Emergency services
are too busy
to worry
about junkies, though.
        Unless they've overdosed.

There's a coach bus
coming tomorrow
to drive people to Tulsa
for free.

We didn't
tell Victor.

If we put him
on the bus alone,
he'd never make it
to rehab.

If I were my dad,
I'd sit
on that bus
with him.
Make sure Victor
checked in
wherever he needed to go.
Stay until
he was released.

But my parents say
they have
a duty
to their church
and community.

There are
18 families
staying
at Uktena Baptist.
They sleep
on floors
in the recreation hall
and in
Sunday School classrooms.

The church
always keeps
supplies on hand
for times
like these.
There are water bottles.
Snack bags.
Canned goods.

Gas lines
to the church kitchen
are unsafe
from storm damage.
But there are
little camping stoves
for families to share.

Each guest
has a sleeping bag
and pillow.
For children
there are toys
and coloring books.
Even diapers
and wet wipes.

A small generator
powers the church
in short stretches.
Gives people time
to plug in
their phones.
Call their friends
and relatives.

My own phone
was found
in our yard.
Chipped
at the corner,
        but still working.

The Wagners and
the Fischers are both
at the church.

The Wagners
survived
by packing
their whole family
into one bathtub.
They have
a few scratches,
but are grateful
        and full of praise.

The Fischers are
less grateful.
They moved here
from Oklahoma City
last year
for teaching jobs.
Never wanted
to be in this town.
And never thanked
my mom
when she set up
their sleeping area.

My parents
        keep bouncing
between our house
and the church.

Our home
is livable,
so we sleep there.

My bedroom,
of course,
is off-limits.
The sign
from the church
is still lodged
into my wall.

There is a beige sofa
and a loveseat
in the living room.

Though Victor and I
are both
about the same height,
I've taken
the loveseat.

I am responsible
for watching
my brother.

Dad never said as much,
but I know
this is the case.

I angle myself
so I can see
his face.

It's lit
by tall red candles
burning
over our mantelpiece.

My brother has water
and saltine crackers
on the table
beside him.
There's a small trash can
in case
he throws up.

His winter coat
is finally off,
but his arms
are hidden
underneath
two thick blankets.
The top blanket
is decorated
with cartoon characters
from *Popeye the Sailor.*

Victor is still
all shivers
and sweats.

He wants to talk.
To stay awake.

My parents
are asleep upstairs.
They've said
their prayers over Victor.
He wasn't calmed.

He keeps chewing
at his lips.

There's no
dead skin there
anymore.
Only a pink pulp.

"I remember
when you were a kid,"
he tells me
    at random.
"Instead of throwing
a tantrum
when you didn't
get your way
you'd stop breathing.
Your face would
go blue.
Then right before
you were about
to pass out,
    you'd breathe."

"I don't remember that
at all,"
I say.

This makes Victor
smile.
As if it gives him
power
to know
I've forgotten
part of my life.

"I do,"
he says,
"You've grown,
buddy.
You don't even have
one cell
in your body
that's the same as
when you were
a toddler.
Weird having
the person you were
disappear,
isn't it?"

I taste death
in his words.
Try to ignore
the flavor.

"Remember
when you were
in middle school
and you had a crush
on that one
cheerleader?"
I ask.

"Which one?"

"You told
Mom and Dad she
was your girlfriend.
They thought
you were too young
for all that.
So they called
the girl's parents.
They were
        confused.
You'd made
the whole thing up."

"Yeah,"
he laughs,
gagging
on the laugh's tail.
"Had to
get better at lying,
        didn't I?
Takes practice,
for sure."

"Weird making the truth
disappear,
isn't it?"
I ask
with bitterness.
The way the Fischers
        spoke to Mom.

"Was that
a dig?"
Victor asks,
head lifting from
his pillow.
"Because you
have the right
        to talk?
I try to be up front
when I can.
But I don't know
half what you hide."

I won't respond.

Victor makes
a choked sound.
Starts hacking
        into his trash bin.

I look up at
a shadowed ceiling fan.
Blades
still.

        Like a model helicopter.

In the morning,
Victor is not
on the sofa.
The trash bin
is tipped over.
His water bottle
is on the floor.

It's early.
I must have
only slept
a few hours.
Yet I'm alert.

If I am my brother's keeper,
I have not kept him
very well.

Upstairs,
I hear Angeline
making her morning cries.

I walk
toward the front door.
Past family photos.
Past little signs
bearing Bible verses.

Through a window,
I can see Victor in
the driveway
next to
our family minivan.

The van
        is running.
He must have found
the keys.

He is staring
at the branches
at our driveway's end.
Maybe wondering
if he can plow into them.
Make it through
the forest.

Some of the wreckage
was cleared from
the road.
Nowhere near enough
for him to make
a clean escape.

He begins to run
his fingers through
his hair and
        pull
            at the roots.

I hear a thud.
Dad comes
bounding downstairs.

He brushes me aside.
Opens the door.
Slams it shut.

I see him yelling
at Victor.
The prodigal son
fallen
from grace
once more.

Dad takes the
keys out of the van.
Places them
        in his pocket.

He and Victor
stand there.
Talking.
Arms swooping.
Lips moving
        too fast to read.

Victor begins slapping
his own face.
He balls his hands
into fists.
Pounds them
into his nose.

Dad grabs at him
to stop
the punching.

Victor
        drops
his arms.

I see blood,
leaking red.
Dripping down
        from Victor's nose.

He sits
on the grass.
Starts sobbing.
His bloodied hands
go back
        to pulling
        at his hair.

Dad walks up
to the door.

"I need to stay in
with Victor,"
he says.
His voice
is gavel-firm.
"I think it's time
for you to be
helpful."

MARIANA

Helpful means
clearing brush
from the road
beside our church.

Others have done
the hardest work
with the saws.
The street is
slowly becoming
walkable.
Part of it
is able to take in
a single lane of cars.

Mom is inside
the church with Angeline.
She keeps the families
comfortable.
Watches over
the children
of other parents
out helping with
the cleanup.

The church runs
the generator
more often now,
since fans are needed.

It's almost 90 degrees.
The sun is
relentless.

The ground
has dried.
Mud has turned back
to dirt.

People are wearing
baseball caps
and headbands.
Some of the men
have their shirts off.
Their sweat
reminds me
of Victor.

There's a red truck
I don't recognize,
parked by
the tree limbs
that block off
the rest of the street.
The flatbed
is full
of poles and pipes.

A man in sunglasses
with tanned skin
is loading
the truck.

A black-haired girl
passes him metal bits
she finds
in the waste.

The girl looks
close to my age.
I've never seen her
in school.

I've been throwing
scraps and sticks
into a wheelbarrow
belonging to the church.

Now I work slower.
Study the girl
with sideways
        glances.

Her features
add up
to a beauty
that makes me feel
        weaker.

The sleeves
on her shirt
are light and loose.
I follow their
movements.
There's a mystery
to them.

It strikes me
as strange.
The shape of
human bodies.
How they move
in space.

I hold
one of my glances
too long.
Her head darts
in my direction.

I look down
at the gray stick
I'm handling.
Toss it into
the wheelbarrow.

When I turn
to find another,
the girl
is beside me.

"You got a name?"
she asks.

Her voice is clipped.
The sound of
the city.

My voice is a
pack of pebbles
falling.

"Philip,"
I say.

She nods in
approval.

"Phil?"

"No, just Philip.
        Phil's an ugly name."

She gives an annoyed
shrug.

"What's the difference?
If you fill
or you fill up?"

"I guess..."

I turn my head left.
Stare at where
the church's sign stood.

"What do you do?"
she asks.

I snap
back to her.

"What do I do?"

"Yeah."

She seems to
think this is
a reasonable question.

"I'm in high school,"
I answer,
which should be
obvious.

"But it's summer vacation,"
she says,
dissatisfied
with my answer.

"Then I vacation,"
I say.

"Some vacation.
Cleaning up
after tornadoes."
She doesn't sound
like she's trying
to be funny.

"Right,"
I say.
Better words
have fallen
out of reach.

I see a piece of pipe
beneath a branch
        and pick it up.

"I better put
this pipe
into this wheelbarrow,"
I say,
as if that makes for
good conversation.

"Why?"
she asks
with real confusion.

"That's where the
heavy trash goes,"
I say.

"But that pipe
isn't trash."

She points to
the red truck.

"Okay…"

I must be
blushing.

"Recycle, boy.
Put it in
my mamá's truck."

I pause at
the order.

"What?
You hate
Mother Nature?"
she asks.

This time,
I have a response.

"You got me.
Mother Nature
isn't my favorite
this week."

"Well, you're breathing,"
is all she says.

She pulls
the pipe
from my hands.

I find another pipe
near the first one.
Snatching it,
I follow her over
to the flatbed.

"You're really rude, man,"
she says,
suddenly upset.

"Why do you
think that?"

"You didn't ask
my name."

"Sorry,"
I say,
meaning it.
"What's your name?"

"Mariana,"
she says
with confidence.
As if it is
the greatest name
ever spoken.

We lay our pipes
on the flatbed.

"So what do you do?"
I ask,
trying to be clever.

"The right thing,"
she says,
with the same
confidence.

"Oh,"
I say,
stomach dropping.
"That's cool."

"I also make necklaces
and bracelets
out of arrowheads
I find in parks."
she says,
more brightly.

"Got any on you?"
I ask.

She is about to answer
when the man
in sunglasses
says something to her
in Spanish.

She responds
with words
I do not know.

"Maybe next time,"
she tells me.

The man,
who must be her relative,
closes up the back
of the truck.
He walks to
the driver's side.

As he gets in,
I see a rosary
        dangling from
        his windshield.

Dad says Catholics
aren't real Christians.
But this only adds
to Mariana's mystery.

"I gotta go,"
she says,
with a rushed seriousness.
"My papá's in the ICU.
You know,
at the hospital?"

"Oh,"
I say,
stomach dropping
again.
"Sorry
to hear that."

Mariana hops into
the passenger side
of the truck.

Before
she shuts the door,
her face twitches.

"Tornadoes, man,"
she tells me.

The truck
        pulls away.

A branch scrapes its side
as it putters off
in clouds of
dust and fumes.

SHEPHERDING

When I get home,
Dad sits silent
at the kitchen table.

"Everything alright?"
I ask.

I immediately
figure
it is not.

Our kitchen
opens out to
the living room.

I see Victor
asleep
on the sofa.
His nose is
bruised
from earlier.
It carries
his snore.

Dad is looking
toward him
as well.

"I think
I'll report
those break-ins
Victor mentioned,"
he whispers.
"This isn't what
I wanted
for my son.
But he needs
help."

I pull out
a chair.
Sit with
my father.

The man is broken up
but doesn't cry.
Never weakens
        his posture.

"I hope you learn
from your brother,"
he says.
"I really do.
When I think of
my children,
I want to be proud.
I'm the shepherd.
Guiding you until
you can guide yourselves.
This is a role
I chose."

I stare at
the wood grain
on the table.

"Your mom and I
helped bring
Victor's light
into this world,"
Dad continues.
"He's an entire soul.
At his age,
I was on fire.
High on
the Spirit of the Lord.
That heat
didn't transfer.
        See how cold
        he is."

I look at
Victor's pulpy lips.
My eyes return to
the wood grain.

Its flow
creates rivers,
with currents
        that run
                in opposite
directions.

"I never thought
I'd reap
what I didn't sow,"
Dad says.
"I never drank
or smoked.
Never hung around
anyone who did drugs.
I thought
the doctors *knew*
what they were doing
with those pills."

"He was
in pain,"
I say,
knowing the excuse
means little.
"They got
it wrong,
trying to help."

"They replaced
a puddle
with an ocean,"
Dad snarls.
"And now we suffer
because
         he suffers."

Victor groans
and gags.
Flutters his lids.

"I am glad he's here,"
Dad insists.
"But I don't know
how to shepherd
my boy
right now."

The groans
grow louder.

Victor thrashes,
flings aside
his Popeye blanket,
        and howls.

Then snores:
        loud-soft,
soft-loud,
        loud-soft,
soft-loud.

HEAVENMAKER

I watch over Victor
while Dad
makes his rounds
at the church.

My phone
is charged.
I'm supposed to call Dad
if Victor
tries anything.

I'm not sure
what "anything"
could mean.

Victor is weak.
But I wouldn't want
to fight him
if he went into
some junkie rage.

When he was
        thrown out
the day after his
high school graduation,
he had a fit.
He didn't hold his
breath
and go blue.

He pushed Mom
into the refrigerator.
Kicked Dad
twice in the shin.

He grabbed
Dad's wallet.
Left it,
        emptied,
in the middle
of the driveway.

Even before Victor
was booted from
the household,
he was known
to steal.

Mom was always
missing jewelry.
Twenty-dollar bills
        disappeared
from her purse.

At first,
she thought
it was just
forgetfulness.

But then Victor
was caught
shoplifting.

He'd been trading
with a girl he knew:
stolen goods
for Oxycontin.
Those pain pills
were even stronger
than Percocet.

While leaving
a Walmart,
a power drill
          popped out
the bottom
of Victor's coat.

It shattered on
the pavement.
Alerted security.

He was ordered
to do community service.
Join a group
for drug abusers
trying to get clean.

The group met
once a week
in the back room of
Uktena's only coffee shop.

It helped Victor.

          For a little while.

The friends Victor made
at his support group
would become
his roommates.

They had connections
in Tulsa
to dope dealers
who didn't bother
with expensive pills.

You could snort,
smoke,
or shoot Tar
and be wired
        for hours.

The crew
made their rent
through pizza delivery
and drive-thru jobs.
Saved enough
to keep their habits up
most months.

They kept Victor
from being homeless
        after he was
        kicked out.

He didn't
need us.

Then one evening
last August,
I was coming back
from Mr. Gregor's cellar.

Victor ran up to me
in the street.

He was
panting.
        Waving
        the arms
of his winter coat.

Uktena is small,
but Victor had kept quiet.
I hadn't seen him
in months.

I was excited
he was there.
To know he hadn't
killed himself.

I heard stories
on the news
of people in Oklahoma
dying from overdoses.
Some dope
had been mixed
with a drug
for putting elephants
        to sleep.

"Getting tall,
my good man,"
Victor said.
"Bet the girls
are going crazy."

Neither of
these things
were true.
He was trying
to warm me up.

He went on
to talk about how
he was
            kicking
his habit.
How he knew
a program
that worked for
a friend.

He just needed
a few dollars
to join it.
Told me
once he was clean,
he'd save up.
Start looking
at jobs out East.
Go to one of the
"Great American Cities."

After high school
ended,
he wanted me
to leave with him.

We'd get an apartment.
Stay together.
Like when we
        were kids.

We'd pig out
on craft beer
        and junk food.
Invite over
women we met
        at clubs and bars.
Work out at gyms
        with rock climbing walls
        and karate classes.
Go to punk shows.
See slasher movies
        on the big screen.

We'd do
everything.

Have all the good things
Mom and Dad
never understood
because they were
        closed
        off.

They saved
all their joys up
for a heaven
that wasn't
there.

Why should
anyone expect
        anything
        after death?

When the brain
crackles off,
you lose
every memory.
Every dream of life.

We had to make heaven
for ourselves.
Here.

That was
the key.

I gave him
$20.
Lied and said
it was my entire pay
from Mr. Gregor.

We agreed to meet
behind the gas station
on the nights
I helped in the cellar.

That way,
Mom and Dad
would never know.

Each time we met,
Victor was thinner.
Paler.

His eyes ping-ponged
as he spoke,
never focusing
for long.

He made
the right promises.

He was in a good program.
Getting clean.
It just took time.
It took
time.

Victor wanted
to show his love.
He could provide
a sip of freedom,
if I was down for it.

I visited
his apartment
that autumn.
Our parents
were in South Korea,
adopting Angeline.

Victor let me sip
my first beer
from a warm can.
It tasted like
sour bread–water.

He kept smiling
and staring
while I drank.
Like he was proud.
I didn't feel
proud.

He didn't
play host long.

Victor made me leave
when Big Gabe entered,
wearing
a tomato-stained polo
from his pizza gig.

They both
were getting jittery.

Big Gabe went into
the bathroom.
I knew he was after
the needles
I found in the
drawer.

I was waved
toward the door.
It shut on me
while I was saying
        goodbye.

I wanted to punch out
the windows
of every car
in the parking lot.
Settled for stomping
on a foam cup
left by the curb.

I puked up
the beer I drank
into some bushes
during my walk home.

My yellow-brown vomit
stuck
like mud
on the leaves.

The heaven that
Victor had made
wasn't
worth
very
much.

LAUGH-LAUGH-LAUGH

Victor wakes me
from my thoughts.

His blankets have fallen
to the floor.
He sits up
with eyes
full
of animal frenzy.

I can see
his bare arms.

"You have a phone,"
he says.

I shrug,
like maybe I don't.
I am holding
the phone
in my hand.

"I need to check in
on my friends,"
he says.

There are seven marks
on each arm.
They look
like scabbed over
bug bites.
With the scabs
        picked off.

"Why?"
I ask.

He is standing
now.

"Why?
Because this
is real here.
You see me?
You see this?"

My grip on
the phone
        is loose
as he comes over
        and pulls it
        from my hand.

"I'll be quick,"
he says.
"Just want to know
how they are."

He is back to
pacing
as he dials.

I hear
Big Gabe
      pick up
      the phone.

I sit down
on my new bed,
the loveseat.

I've failed
again.
I cannot keep
my brother
from doing anything.

The volume on the phone
is high enough
to hear
every word.

Big Gabe is in Tulsa.
He took
the coach bus,
which came and went,
three hours ago.

He can barely speak,
because the Tar
is hitting him hard.

He's only shot up
one time,
but he's good.
He's great.
He's at home
in the world again.

He's on the grass
in a park.
Resting in peace.
He can't get up.
Can't drive.

     Not now.
          Tomorrow.
     He'll come
          tomorrow.

He'll need cash
to make up for the ride.

     But he'll
          come tomorrow.
     He'll come.
     You bet,
          you bet.

The sweat on
Victor's forehead
is dripping more
than before.

He shines
with both hope
and hunger,
so close to
healing.

"You can't,"
I say.

Victor isn't
listening.

I hold my breath in.
Try to go back
to my toddler self.
The effort is
forced
and fake.

I start breathing again
the moment
the pressure
starts to bother me.

Victor is off
the phone.

The animal frenzy
in his eyes
has grown.

"You knew about that bus?"
he asks.

"It doesn't matter."
I say.

"You knew.
Of course you knew.
My family wants
to send me
off the cliff.
Even you."

"I don't want
anything,"
I say.

"Then you're not
a person,"
he says.
"Of course
you want me to be
whatever *you* want.
So I can
pluck you
out of here.
Take you down
to Paradise City."

Victor rocks
with fury.

"It must be lonely
in this house,"
he growls.
"So sad.
So sorry
about that."

The room
seems to slip away.
Like the death cloud
has returned.

Victor continues.
"But you can
go to h—"

I find myself
laughing.
The laughs
are warm,
running hot
through my
cheekbones.

The joke
that is my life
and the life of
every person
I've met
is too much
not to laugh at.

I was right
to wish for
the wind to
blow it all away.
Only wrong in how
I felt about it.

I should have
laughed.
Seen how funny
this was
and laughed
until I was bluer
        than any
        toddler tantrum
        made me.

Laughed at
the swirling clouds.
Laughed at
the marks
on Victor's arms.
Laughed at
the door
in Mr. Gregor's throat.
Laughed at
the faith of my parents
in a world where
everything
disappeared
no matter what
you did.

All of my skin
will soon be
dead skin.
Floating on
a planet
that will die
one day.
When there'll be
no days
or nights
or anything
at all.

I laugh.
Laugh–laugh–laugh
      at the joke
         I've fallen into.

I know
why Victor
smiled at the teenage actors
murdered
on his laptop screen.

He was in
on the joke.

And just as I am
going to tell him this,
what I've learned,
he hits me.
      Swings hard
         into my
         laughing cheekbones.

"This isn't funny,"
he says.
"I'm burning.
My whole body
is burning
down."

The sting on my cheek
returns me
to the room.

My brother is shaking.

There are tears
caught up in his sweat.

His pain is
deeper than
the joke.

More than any laugh
can cover up.

PART III

THE

BLACK

DOORS

NOTHING
GETS
FORGOTTEN

I've decided not
to tell Dad
about the call
with Big Gabe.
I can't let Victor
suffer this way.

I'm not strong enough
to stop him.
Maybe it isn't
my place to.

I slept two hours
last night.
Kept thinking
my awful thoughts
about death and Victor.
The painful joke
and the laughing pain.
Don't want to think
anymore.

Today,
I have to be helpful,
of course.

There are houses
to repair
and rebuild.
Roads to
finish clearing.

Everyone is volunteering
to help everyone else.
They bring their tools
and their skills.
Their willingness to
bring back
what was
destroyed.

I want
their spirits.
Simple,
but so much more
than what's
inside me.

A local store
the tornado missed
has donated lumber.
We can start
bringing the flattened houses
back to life.

I nail
wood planks together.
Make new wall frames
alongside
two other men.

They seem joyful.
Talk about football.
          Politics.
                    Past hunting trips.

They ask questions.
Try to include me.
I stay quiet mostly.
Keep hoping
the red truck will return
          with Mariana
               in it.

She frightens me.
Yet in the
twisted thoughts
of last night,
when my mind turned
to her,
I felt
some flutter
within me.
It was more beautiful
than sad.

There was
          a weight
          in that beauty.
Like I wasn't living up
to what it needed
me to be.

My world
is tornadoes and Tar
and death
no one dodges.
Still I see neighbors
thanking God
they're here.

They pick up
their tools
and put together
        what the winds
                ripped apart.

A few hours
into my work,
the red truck comes.

Mariana's in
the passenger seat
with the window
rolled down.
She gives
        a salute.

My throat tightens
as I salute back.

She leaves
the truck.

Walks
straight to me.

The men
I'm working with
notice.
They stop talking
and grin.

I must be as red
as the truck
Mariana came out of.

"*Hola*, stranger,"
she says.

She's wearing a
light blouse with
flowers on it.
And an arrowhead necklace
I know she must
have made.

Black garbage bags
        stick out
of her blue jean pockets.

"Hey,"
I say.
"Back for more?"

My worker friends
tell me
they have the frames
under control,
if I want to take
a walk.

At first,
I don't go for
the offer.

Mariana
frowns.

I change
my mind.

"Let's go get
some of these yards
cleaned up,"
she says.
"I brought
extra bags."

We hold
two bags each.
Scraps
and splinters
go in one.
Objects to keep
go in the other.

"How's your dad?"
I ask.

She puts a
dented dog bowl
into her
keep bag.

"My papá,
he was driving
his semi on I-44,
from Oklahoma City
to Tulsa,
when the tornado
        flipped him
right over."

"What?
The storm went up
that far?"

"Uh-huh,"
she says.
"There were a few
twisters.
The big one
that hit here
was more than
a mile wide.
Went 200 miles an hour."

I've been too worried
about Victor
to look into facts
about the storm.

"Is your dad
okay?"

"His face is
in a cast,"
she says.
"Maybe
he won't have
the same face
when they take it off."

I stop
walking.

"I'm so sorry..."

She gazes at the sky,
following the flight
of a kingbird.

"He's alive.
And that means
there's a reason
he's still with us."

Mariana lets down
her bags.
Begins to sniffle.

I want to touch
her arm.
Or hug her.
I'm not sure
if she'd like that.

"I don't know why you're out here.
You should be
        with your dad."

She shakes
her head.

"No, I can't be
in there that long.
I can't.
My brother and I,
we gotta
get out
of our heads."

"So you go
and pick up
other people's
garbage?"

"No...
We can reuse things.
Recycle.
And the real garbage
needs to get cleared by
somebody.
We're in the area.
There are people here
who've lost more
than us."

"That's very
unselfish,"
I say.

She wipes her nose
on her sleeve.

"This is what
we were put here for,"
she says.
"What we do
        matters
        forever, man."

Compared to
that kind of responsibility,
the idea of life
as a terrible joke
seems comforting.
I change
        the topic.

"So you live
around here?"

"Nah.
Not too far.
Tulsa."

"You like living
in the city?"

"It can be alright,"
she says,
picking
her bags back up.
"It can be
        lonely."

We're walking
again.

I put
a cracked clock
        in my *keep* bag.

"Why?"
I ask.
"You don't have trouble
talking to people."

Mariana snorts.

"Man, I have
so many troubles
talking to people.
        You don't even know."

"That's a lie."

"I never lie.
I live my life
like I'm under oath."

"That's a lie, too."

"No, really.
        I never lie."

"So if I asked
you a question,
you'd tell me
        the truth?"

This seems
like a good way
        to fish around
        her mind.

"Or not say anything,"
she says.
She picks up
a naked Barbie doll,
blonde hair
gone brown
from dirt.

"Fair enough,"
I tell her.

I'd like to ask
what she thinks
of me.
If she wants
to kiss.
My heart rate
        spikes
at the thought.

"Are you ever afraid
of anything?"
I ask instead,
in a way that seems clumsy.

She
arches
her eyebrows.

"I get afraid,
but don't let it stay.
Why?
        You afraid?
Too many twisters
out here?"

I typically say
as little as I can
get away with.

Speaking always
makes me feel
like I'm shedding
        clothes.

Now,
in front of Mariana
and her
arched eyebrows,
I feel pulled
to speak.

"Sometimes,
I'm afraid
every part of me
is wrong.
I don't know
what to believe
        about life.
                Or death.
                        Or anything.

I just live.

                But for what?
So I can move
somewhere else maybe.
With more lights and motion.
        Find a girl.
        Go to parties.
        Do something
                to forget I'm afraid.

I'm 16.

I feel like
I'm 100,
on my deathbed,
        hooked up to a machine
        thinking:
                I blew it,
                        I wasted it.
What does
that even
mean?"

There's a
pinch in my chest.

Though my words
spin
        and spray,
what I'm saying
is real.

It's where I am
        right now.

"Life's
all around me,"
I say.
"I just don't know
        what to do with it."

Mariana
is picking at
her arrowhead necklace.
Not smiling
or frowning.

"Sorry to dump
all that nonsense,"
I tell her.
"It's not right,
with your dad
and everything."

Mariana's
eyebrows
        lower.

She pokes
my shoulder
with the garbage bag
still in
her hand.

"You are
messed up,
boy."
she says.

    "I like it."

WASTED

There's a jump
in my step
as I jog over debris
to our house.

I catch a glow
from our yellow siding
        and dusty windows.

The bite the tornado
took out of
our top floor
is charming somehow.

I don't mind
that my bedroom
has a balcony
        that shouldn't be there.

I'm excited
to tell Victor
I've gotten
a phone number.
That I've met someone.

Maybe we can
connect
on this.

It could distract him
from his
hunger.

When my sneakers
hit the welcome mat,
the glow inside me
drops.

My parents
open the door.

Mom's been crying.
Her eyes are
strained
and pink at the edges.

"Here's our Brother of the Year,"
Dad says,
his voice less
like a gavel
and more like
        a sledgehammer.

I enter.

Victor is
still there
in the living room.

Angeline must be
in her crib.

"We've been having
a wonderful chat
with Victor,"
Dad says.
"He tried to take
the phone
right out
of my hand.
Do you know why
he might want
the phone, Philip?"

I want to fade
into the floor.

"You going to
answer?
You going to be
the man here?"

"I don't know,"
I mumble.

"You don't know.
That makes sense.
That's honest.
Well, I don't know
why I was
punished
with children like this.
I guess that's just my
cross to bear."

Dad looks at Victor,
then turns
back to me.

"I'm ashamed
to have sons
who are
        liars
        and sneaks.
This isn't how
we raised you.
But you make
        your own choices.
And you've chosen
to be burdens
to the world
instead of gifts.

        Congratulations."

"Andrew…"
Mom says,
trying to soften my father
        by using
        his first name.

But I deserve
every
cut.

"Victor's told us
about your
little meetups
after you went to
Matt Gregor's place,"
Dad says.

Each word
burns
through
me.

"Gregor wouldn't
have given you
        a dime
if he knew
what you did
with his money,"
Dad continues.
"He was investing
in your future.
In college.
He saw so much
        in you.
You failed
that good man."

In a flash,
I see Mr. Gregor.
A corpse in my mind
with a
raw
                red
                        throat.

"This whole time,
you weren't
looking out for
your brother,"
Dad hisses.
"You
hated
him."

My face must
give off
a question.

I have
never
hated Victor.

"Yes,
        hated."
Dad says.
"You didn't show love.
Love isn't some
        feel-good goo.
I love you all more
than my heart
can stand.
But I don't feel
a splat
of goo.

Love seeks
what's good
for another.
What's best
for their life.
Even if
it hurts
in the short term."

Mom
slumps
        over
the kitchen counter.

"You were going
to let your brother
get more drugs,"
Dad says,
        slapping down
        his palm.
Almost pinning
Mom's hair.

"You were going
to let someone
        come here
and give him
        that stuff.
But you know what?
Victor's buddy, Gabe —
he's dead now.
        He's dead.
        He OD'd."

"Cops found his body
in Chandler Park,
over in Tulsa.
Gabe's mom –
she's been staying
at the church
because her house
        got blown up
        by a tornado.
And now she has
to bury her son.
That's a whole life,
sacred to God,
        wasted."

Victor has dug
his head
into a pillow.

I could dig
my head
into the center
of the earth.

"That might have been
your brother,"
Dad says,
his words
slowing.

My mother's
sobs
soak up
the silence.

I am nerves,
firing blind
into thick air.

Drained
of every word
and
every solid thought.

OLDER

There's no
punishment
to line up
with what I've done.

I've lost
the right to
my phone.
Mainly to keep
my brother from it.

Dad thinks
Victor's about
a day or so away
from getting better.

He's still not
holding down food.

Mom brings him
bottles of water
from our pantry.

She whispers
to Victor
that he is *close*.

It will soon
be over.

He'll be
better.

He just has to stay
better.

She wonders,
since the roads
are clearer,
if we should get him
to the hospital.
It's smarter to
use doctors
than to go
      "cold turkey."

For now,
Victor stays
with us.

I see strands of gray
in Mom's hair.
She can't yet
re-dye it.

With water cut off,
we haven't showered
since the storm.

We clean ourselves
with bars of soap
and water from jugs.

We do have
a travel toilet.
It helps,
between Angeline's
dirty diapers
and the diarrhea
Victor has.

My family
was prepared
for this disaster.

I would only
have let it
wash over me.

I've counted on
their love
without knowing
how much energy
that love takes.

As Victor rests,
Mom does
muscle exercises
with Angeline's
arms and legs.

She makes sure
her daughter has
the body tone
she needs
to grow
at the right pace.

I'll never understand
why my parents
flew across an ocean
to take on
a child
with such needs.

The weight and the work
they accepted
isn't only because of
back-patting
from the church.

Mom says she felt
called.

She wanted to do this
before she was
too old.

As her hands
squeeze the dough
of Angeline's legs,
the child giggles.

"You're such a happy baby,"
Mom says
in kid-speak.
"A happy-happy baby.
        Yes, you are.
Know who else
        was a happy baby?"

"Your brother, Victor,"
Mom says,
cutting
the kid-speak.
"He was a happy
little boy, too.
Made all sorts
of things
with Mega Bloks.
            Didn't you,
            Victor?"

Victor is facing
the inside of
the sofa.
I don't know
if he's awake.

"He'd come over.
Pull on my shirt.
Say:
Look, Mommy,
this is how you build
an outer space ship.
Look, Mommy,
            this is how you build
            an Evil France Tower.
Look, Mommy,
            this is how you build
            the biggest big-house
            that you put
            the world inside."

"Remember how he did
those models
with you,
          Philip?"
Mom asks.
"Dad and I thought
he might be
an engineer."

I look up
at the ceiling fan.
Picture it spinning,
faster
and faster.

Maybe
none of us
should have gotten
older.

Or maybe
we're still just kids,
building our lives
out of the blocks
we've been given.

Angeline looks at me,
eyes alive
with excitement.

I am already
older
than I ever
want to be.

DROP

It's evening,
maybe seven o'clock,
and all of us
are tired.

Angeline has
fallen asleep
on a blanket.
Mom is
lying beside her.

Dad stays
in range
because he does not
trust Victor alone
anymore.

He nods off
in an armchair,
head falling
to the side.
He even
drools some,
like Angeline does.
Shows the child
        inside the man.

He destroyed
something in me today.
Perhaps it needed
    to tumble.

After more
hacking
and heaving,
Victor
    drifted off.

None of us
have slept
regular hours.

I find myself
    in and out
of black patches
    of sleep.

Memories
of Victor and I
gluing together models
    cross into
Mom reading us
bedtime stories
about Oklahoma's pioneers.

I see myself riding
a covered wagon
through the Great Plains
    into mystery,
finally settling here
    on this loveseat.

I wake
to Mom screaming.
Dad bounding.
The ceiling fan
glaring with its
one eye.

"Where is she?
      Where is she?
            Where is she?
      Where is she?"

Angeline's blanket
is empty.

So is Victor's spot
at the sofa.

"No-no-no.
      Where is she?"

Mom is looking
under the sofa,
as if that might
make sense.

Dad bursts
down the hallway.
Out the
front door.

I'm locked in place,
trying to process
      what is happening.

"Were we all
asleep?"
I ask.

"Yes,"
Mom's voice
fires in panic.
"My baby…
Where is she?"

We jump from
room to room.
Frantic and confused.
Checking
and re-checking.

We look in cabinets
and closets.
In the basement
and up the stairs.
My legs move
without thinking
and my eyes
          scan and search
          and pour through
                    every space.

My hands and feet
claw and kick
through the heaps
of drywall
and insulation
inside of my
room's broken belly.

I pull up
the sign in my wall.
Look
beneath it.

Nails
cut into my hands.
Thin trickles
of blood
run down
my wrists.

I am waiting to find
her body.
Like the victim
of a bombing,
buried in the rubble.
Under layers
of decay.
Still breathing.
        Hoping to be found.

Wires scrape
my forehead.
The search
takes me closer
to the edge
of my balcony.

I peer into
the falling dark.
The air tastes bitter
in my mouth.
Like vinegar.

The battered bones
of Uktena
reach up from
the ground
into the gray-blue sky.

The streets
are quiet,
but I see a shadow
up the road.

It darts
through
the growing darkness.
It seems to hold
a rounded lump.

I bite into
the air.
Place my
bloodied palms
onto a wooden beam,
                    jutting outward.

Slivers slice
into me
as I slide
        down.

Letting go,
I drop
into
the wind.

CAVE

My legs and ankles
ignore the impact
of the ground.
I trip forward
from the grass
into the road.

Dim stars
and a slit moon
show me along
the path I know.

The shadow of Victor
has turned,
but I see
the direction it took.
I leap over trash piles.
Around hills
of brush.

I pass the gas station,
its pumps covered
in tarp ghosts.

I head where the roads
turn from blacktop
to gravel.

I can see the outlines
of Victor's footprints
in the
scattered stones.

I hear a creak
and the cold slam
of steel doors
in a field ahead,
where Mr. Gregor's house
once stood.

The ruins
of his home
are shot through
with stars.

My breath
runs along the pull
of the breeze.

Beside a crumbled wall,
the black rectangles
of two doors appear.

The cellar.

I grab at the latches.
Ribbons
of caution tape
are already removed.

I pull open
the doors that
have cut
and killed.

I call into
the darkness.

"Victor?
Victor?"

I hear a rustle,
which could be
my brother.
Or an animal.
Or a demon
that the storm
brought into
our world.

The dark is deep
and seems to swirl.
To take me into
          its black hole.

In it,
a little cry comes,
muffled by what
must be Victor's hand.

I know that
he is there,
Angeline squirming
in his arms.

I take careful steps
down
into
the earth.

The black doors
shut behind me.

I am
lost
in my pictured
        Nothingness.

As I reach
the bottom,
I remember
the lanterns
Mr. Gregor kept
on the far wall.

My blind fingers
feel for them.
They curl along
the dark,
touching
wet and winding
shapes.

Victor's rustling
is closer
and I hear his
breath flowing
into the black.

"What are you doing,
Victor?"
I ask the darkness.

The darkness breathes
but does not
answer.

My fingers swim
further,
hunting for a lantern.

"I'm here for you,"
I say.
"I'm here."

Landing on
a glass form,
my fingers glide
down
to a switch.
A shower of light
enters my eyes.

Victor comes into
my view.
One arm is wrapped
around Angeline.
The other shields
his lids
from the light.

He is near the
cellar steps.

I race to the doorway
     to block
       his path.

As he lowers his arms
from his eyes,
I see he has
a yellow notepad
and a pencil
in his hand.

There are
scribblings
on the pad's first page
I can't read.

Angeline is blinking
at the light.
Victor half-covers
her mouth.

I'm scared he'll
smother her.
She breathes
through her nose,
     fast with fear.

"Why?"
I ask,
staring into
the skull
that is
my brother's face.

"It's not a big deal,"
he mumbles,
     rocking slightly.
"You'll get her back."

Victor leans into
a rack of bagged clothes.
Almost knocks
it over.

"No,"
I tell him.
"Please.
Give me Angeline."

I puff out my chest.
Try to make sure
he doesn't run
up the stairs.

"Let me finish the note,"
Victor says,
     rocking harder.
"They've got to
understand.
They give me
maybe five hundred bucks.
Not much of
a ransom.
Don't have to get
police involved."

"They've probably
already called them,
Victor,"
I say.
"This is their daughter.
Your *sister.*

        This won't work."

"What will?"
Victor is shouting now,
waving the pad
and pencil.
"Tell me,
and I'll do that.
How far do
I get
sucked
down
before any of you
see?"

Angeline's tiny feet
keep bumping
against Victor.
She's trying
to get free.
Her eyes,
so sad and sharp,
look into mine.

Victor is swaying.
Like he's tipsy.
Or about to speak
        in tongues.

"You're going to
have to ride
the pain,"
I tell him.
"It'll be better.
You want all
your days to be like
the past year?
Until you just fall
        apart?"

"Yes,"
he says,
spitting.
"Yes, I want that."

"You didn't,"
I say,
trying to speak
carefully.
"You liked to
build things.
To put them
together.
You didn't want
to tear yourself
        apart
or take all of us
        down."

Victor's pad slips
from his grasp
as he beats on
the wall.

"Building,
        tearing,
it doesn't matter,"
he says.
"Can't judge it
one way
or the other.
It's not better
or worse.
Life doesn't
care about
your thoughts.
And I don't care either.
This is just
        what has
        to be."

"You don't
believe that,"
I say.

I am watching
Angeline,
looking for an opening.
Some way I can get her
        from his grip.

Her head is
too close
to the concrete wall.

Victor's swaying
is only
speeding up.

"It doesn't matter
what I believe,"
he says.
"You follow
        the burn
        inside.
Do what
it asks.
That's all.
No law in
the universe
        says
        anything more.
You need to
accept that.
To
let
go."

Victor teeters
forward.
His knees
        bend.
Like he is trying
to sit.
To fold Angeline
        into
        himself.

The faces of
my sister and brother
strike me
with an
electric focus.

Every detail
of the cellar
seems to pop
and glow with life.

A power surges
through my nerves.
Like the light
exploding from
the bulb of the
lantern.

"I'm not leaving,
Victor,"
I say,
with calm
beyond
my understanding.
"Say what
you want,
but you matter to me.
Angeline matters to me.
This isn't just
some thought
in the wind
or feel-good goo.

I love you."

Victor laughs
        the laugh that lives
                inside of death.

This is the laugh
he struck me out of.
Now he's landed
        in its
        spiral.

He places Angeline
gently onto
the cellar floor.
My gut flutters
at the hopeful sound
        of her weeping.

Victor looks
into me
with a fire
that screams
with more than
animal frenzy.

"Brother,"
he says,
the death laugh
on his lips.
"You are so lucky
to think
that love
could ever be
even close to
enough."

In a sudden
    jerk,
the pencil
he holds
begins jumping
        in and out
                of his right arm.

The tip stabs
        into his scabs,
and into places
        where no marks
        had been.

The pencil jabs
at skin,
both living
and dead.

Jets of red
        spurt
        and pump.

The blood arches
out from
the leaking lines
of his veins.
Splashes onto my
        shirt,
        as I try to
                pull the pencil away.

He hits
my thumb
      with
            the tip.

Our blood
swaps
      and mixes.

We go down
      in a blur,
knocking against
shelving.
Against Mr. Gregor's
old picture frames.

There is a crack
      and a howl
as everything
seems to break
around us.

We are infants
in the womb.
Floating
in the hot red
of an underwater cave.

I will not
let go
of my brother.

RIGHT

I spent a night
in the same hospital
as Mariana's father.

The man in the bed
behind the curtain
near me
groaned constantly.
Yet my sleep
was long
and dreamless.

My head and hands
are bruised.
Dotted with
little lines.

Both Victor and I
were bandaged
by my father.
He used Mr. Gregor's
first aid kits.

Dad heard shouts
and pounding
as he searched
the streets.
He'd gone left
instead of right
when he first
went outside
to look for Angeline.

The blue-and-red lights
of the cop cars
he'd called for
were almost there
when our sounds
rose in the night.

He found his sons
bundled together
beside his daughter's
screams.

Victor passed out
before me
as we tussled.
Sank into
the red wine
of our own sweat
and blood.

My brother will be
here,
in this hospital,
much longer
than I will.

I'm officially released
but visit him
before leaving.
Stand alongside
my ever-tired parents.

They were afraid
he might die,
between the dehydration
and blood loss.

Strung up with an IV,
color returns
to his sleeping face.
It's softer now.
Less deadened.
More free.

Mom sits next
to his bed,
Angeline on her lap.

I wouldn't let Angeline
in the same room
as Victor.
Even if soldiers
guarded the child.

But this is Mom's way
of saying
she forgives him.

Dad talks to a doctor,
a man in his forties
wearing a yarmulke.

"Thoughts on pain relief
are changing,"
the doctor says.
"People were
convinced
it was a human right
not to suffer pain.
God knows,
if there's anything
that isn't a right,
        it's that.
It's good to
ease pain,
most certainly.
        But not
        at this cost.
You need to get to
the root.
Not just cover pain
with drugs."

Dad's head
        bobs
with the man's
sentences.

The doctor
points his clipboard
in Victor's direction.

"We won't be
placing your son
on any opioids.
His arms
will be sorer,
but *he* will be
          better."

My spirit
is with Victor
and his recovery.
But I am distracted.

I found out
Mariana's papá
was here
when I saw her pass
the door
of my hospital room
with her mother
and brother.
They held
golden balloons
and purple flowers.
Walked faster
than I could react.

I'm itching
to find Mariana,
if she's still around.

I slip out
of Victor's room
as Dad continues
chatting with the doctor.

I peep through
each of
the open doors.
Try to play cool.

When I see balloons
in one room,
I get struck
with a giddy fear.
Then notice
Mariana's family
isn't there.

Finally,
I hear her voice.
Ringing
down the hall.

I don't know
if I should be doing
what I want to.
Dropping in on
their family moment.

I've never met
her parents
and I'm not sure
how to explain
the shape I'm in.

I stop next to
a vending machine.
Study the prices.

Just as I begin
to get hungry,
Mariana comes out
of a doorway.

"What?"
she cries.
"You stalking me, boy?"

"No,"
I say,
grinning.
"My brother's here."

"You didn't tell me
the tornado got him,"
she says.

She looks at
my bandages.
"And got you, huh?"

"There's been
another one?"
I ask.

"Somewhere,
probably,"
she says.

She rubs what
looks like
another arrowhead necklace.

"You want
a hug?"
she asks.

This stuns me.

I've never been
hugged by
anyone
who wasn't in
my family.

My lungs
tighten
as her body
surrounds me.

I can smell
flowers
in her hair.

I pat her shoulders.
She holds
the hug
and the pressure
        dissolves me.

Then she
pushes back.

"Man, you're
a terrible hugger."

There's a laugh
in my voice
as I respond.

It's the right kind
of laugh.

It puts me where
    I want to be.

EPILOGUE

The sign
from the church
was thrown away
when we finally
cleaned my bedroom.

Our insurance
will help us
rebuild.

Soon I won't
be sleeping
        in the living room.

The new sign
on the church's lawn
is made of stone.
It holds
the same verse
from the Book of Revelation:

BEHOLD,
I MAKE ALL THINGS NEW

We hope Victor
is being made new.
He's in
a private clinic.

At the dinner table,
a ghost still sits
in his chair.

Dad's looking into
college programs
for him.
Mostly related
to engineering.

"The boy
needs something
to point his arrow at,"
he says.

There's a real risk
of Victor relapsing.
The doctors worry
about his pattern
of self-harm.

Mom writes Victor
letters by hand
each week.
She tells him about
the town's recovery.

I wish you were here
to say
"Look, Mommy,
     this is how you build
     a town,"
she wrote in one letter.
Maybe one day,
you'll help build up
     places like ours.

For now,
we're just glad
Victor is alive.
Deaths from heroin
went up
in Oklahoma
after Big Gabe passed.

Police officers
and firefighters
are keeping Narcan
in their vehicles.
They inject this drug
into overdose cases.
It gives addicts
another chance
to live.
To get clean.

Most never do.

Many of the people dying
weren't looking
for trouble.
Their doctors
gave them pills
for actual problems.
Drug companies
promised doctors
the pills
were not addictive.

They were.

Life presses on,
through the lies
we weave around it.

Uktena's streets
are fully cleared.

Soon
we'll begin
another year
of school.

I'm trying to stretch out
these last days
of summer
by seeing Mariana.

It's over an hour drive
from Uktena
to Tulsa.

Sometimes
we meet
halfway for fast food.
Other times,
I go out to the city
or she comes here
for dinner.

Her family's home
is decorated
with haloed angels
and Catholic saints.

Mariana teaches me
Spanish words.
She laughs at
how I say them.
Her family also
finds my speech funny,
but they are kind.

Her papá has
jagged scars
from the accident.

When he came
out of the hospital,
her mamá
held a feast.

She calls
her husband's survival
a miracle.
Lights candles
before an image of
the Blessed Virgin
near her television.

Were others,
like Mr. Gregor,
less blessed,
I wonder?
Swept away
by the summer's storms.
Thrown out
of this great mystery.

When Mariana
visits my family,
Dad bombards her
with questions.
Which she hates.
        She's used to doing
        the question-asking.

Mom says
she likes Mariana.
I know she thinks
I'm too young
to be dating.

My parents insist
we're never
alone together
behind a closed door.

Tonight,
it's just me,
my mother and father,
and Angeline,
under electric lights.
Our power has
returned.

Droplets slide down
the cool glass of
our windows.
Rain taps the rooftop
of the shelter
that is
our home.

As we sit at
our table to dine,
our prayers
wheel around us.

I shut my eyes.

I push myself
as deep as I can
into darkness.

I try to return
to the thick black
of the cellar
where Victor
      was found.

I push past
the thoughts
that flicker and fade.
Move through
the sound
of my parents' voices.

Let myself sink
      into
      a wordless warmth.

The buzz of the phone
in my father's pocket
echoes
in the quiet
of this dark.

I open
my eyes.

When the prayer finishes,
Dad pulls out
the phone
to check it.

He twitches
and tucks in his lips.
Holds up the
glowing screen
for us to see.

Blasted in red letters
is a message
for our area:

> *Emergency*
> *Alert*

Angeline giggles
at the table's
strange
and sudden silence.

I shut my eyes
again.

WANT TO KEEP READING?

If you liked this book, check out another book

from West 44 Books:

NOT HUNGRY
BY KATE KARYUS QUINN

ISBN: 9781538382691

I'M A LIAR

A liar who tells only one lie.

The same one
      again
            and
                  again.

As I skip lunch
for the third time
that week.

Or pass on the tub of popcorn
—the biggest they offer—
as it travels between
  my sister,
            my mom,
                  and I.

Or pick at
a piece of pizza
  before
      tossing it
            in the
                  trash.

In all these situations
the same
      three
            words
                  work.

Check out more books at:
www.west44books.com

An imprint of Enslow Publishing

WEST 44 BOOKS™

ABOUT THE AUTHOR

Ryan Wolf works as a grant writer for nonprofits in the Chicago area. He holds a master's degree in the humanities from the University of Chicago, as well as a bachelor's degree in English, communication studies, and creative writing. Ryan has previously published work in *The Buffalo News* and *Conversations on Jesuit Higher Education*. He lives in Oak Park, Illinois, with his wife, Jenna.